THE BLACK BELT CLUB

Seven Wheels
of Power

The dojo at Karate Kids World

THE BLACKBELT CLUB

Seven Wheels of Power

DAWN BARNES

illustrated by
BERNARD CHANG

SCHOLASTIC INC.

New York Toronto London Auckland Sydney
Mexico City New Delhi Hong Kong Buenos Aires

This book is being published simultaneously in hardcover
by the Blue Sky Press.

ISBN-13: 978-0-439-63936-1
ISBN-10: 0-439-63936-0

Text copyright © 2005 by Dawn Barnes
Illustrations copyright © 2005 by Scholastic Inc.

Special thanks to Robert Martin Staenberg.

12 11 10 9 8 7 6   7 8 9 10 11 12/0
Printed in the United States of America   40
First Scholastic paperback printing, March 2005

*To Bonnie and Robbie for presenting
a mirror of inspiration.*

*To Ben for being the wall
on which it hangs.*

—D. B.

For my mom, Theresa.

*With special thanks to Bonnie,
Dawn, Kadir, Thom, and Kathy.*

—B. C.

CHAPTER 1

SENSEI HAS called a three o'clock meeting of the Black Belt Club—a "special workshop," she said. I know what that means—we're going on a mission, and this will be my first. We'll be practicing the Four Winds Kata—the one I just learned. I've had lessons every day for three weeks, and now I can do it. The others all know it perfectly.

I'm starting to feel anxious. That's because I'm new to the BBC. And I'm just not sure why I got invited into the Black Belt Club anyway.

Three weeks ago, I got a letter in the mail that read:

THE BLACK BELT CLUB

Max Greene,

CONGRATULATIONS! You have been officially invited into the BLACK BELT CLUB. Out of 900 students at Karate Kids World, only 4 students were invited into the Black Belt Club.

You must promise to show Patience, Focus, Kindness, Honesty, and Respect at all times, especially at home, in school, and at the dojo.

You must promise to be available for special workshops in order to help make the world a better place for all people.

Most important, you must promise to always Try Your Best and to Never Give Up.

-Sensei Dawn

KARATE KIDS WORLD

Go figure?

I can see why the other kids are members, because they're really good! But me? Basically, I'm a klutz. Uncoordinated. Clumsy.

Sensei tells me to always think positive thoughts, but the truth is, I'm just not very sure of myself. "Max," my uncle Al says, "you've done enough karate. Why don't you try something that *matters*? Like football," he tells me all the time. But I don't care. I'm only stuck with Uncle Al until Dad finishes his work in China.

If I can get past the panic and slow down for a minute, the truth of the matter is I *do* want to go to Sensei's special workshop. And I *do* want to be in the Black Belt Club. It's a huge honor.

So on the day of the workshop, I brushed my teeth, combed my hair, and put on my *gi*.

I like the black *gi*, the uniform we all wear when we join the Black Belt Club. It has draw-string pants and a kimono top.

Everyone's top came with an animal patch sewn on the back of it—except mine. Sensei asked me what my Animal Power was, but I didn't know. So she said to tell her when it comes to me. What does that mean? Will it visit me in a dream or something? I hope it's cool, like a tiger, and not wimpy, like an earthworm. That would be my luck—Max Greene, Animal Power: worm.

I reached for my BBC pack. Maybe the workshop today won't be so difficult. We'll see. After all, this is a *special*, special workshop because it's the Black Belt Club!

When I got my invitation three weeks ago, I couldn't wait to tell my uncle. I ran downstairs for breakfast with my invitation in my hand.

I sat down, carefully placing my letter on the table in front of me. I was waiting for my uncle to notice and ask me about it. But he didn't. That's just the way he is. Finally, I handed him the letter. "Here, Uncle Al," I said.

He grabbed the envelope. He began reading it aloud. He never does that. Then he smiled. I could tell he was proud of me. He finished reading the letter, and then he looked up. I was smiling, too, ready for his praise. But instead, he began to laugh.

WHY ARE YOU LAUGHING?

CAN YOU IMAGINE? INVITED INTO *THE BLACK BELT CLUB*?

IT'S A REALLY *COOL* THING.

ONLY FOUR KIDS GET INVITED.

"Come on, Max. Who are you trying to kid?" he asked. "You'd better take this to your teacher and tell her to give it to the right Max." He tossed the letter across the table and turned back to his newspaper.

I picked up the invitation and walked out the door.

CHAPTER 2

I ENTERED the karate school and saw only the three other BBC kids in the dojo. The dojo is the room where we do our karate. It always seems bigger when it's not filled with students. I looked through the glass doors at the mirrored walls of the dojo. Seeing myself in my uniform and my black belt, for a split second, I felt special. After all, I had to train hard for six years to get to my black belt. But then I looked at the other three kids. They were warming up, and all of them were smart and confident.

I'd known them all for years, from our karate classes together. Even though I'd been practicing the Four Winds Kata for the three weeks since the invitation came, who was I kidding? Today I could see Uncle Al was right. I didn't belong in any Black Belt Club.

Through the glass door, Sensei smiled at me and beckoned. I bowed and entered the dojo.

"Well, it's just that my uncle told me you made a mistake because, you know, I'm not really that good." I felt nervous with everyone watching me.

"Turn to the class, Max." We faced the other kids.

"Everyone, this is our newest member in the Black Belt Club. Please clap for Max."

My stomach tightened with excitement. "You mean I'm really good enough to be in the Black Belt Club? I can't believe it!"

"Line up with the other students now, so we can start our special workshop."

I stood straight in line with the other kids and felt nervous and happy at the same time.

It was obvious why the other three kids in line were in the club.

Antonio is only ten, but everyone knows he never gives up. And he never complains. He just practices and practices until he gets it. In one week, Antonio can learn a kata that has taken me a month to master, no kidding. And the moves of his kata are as graceful as a dance.

Maia is the same age as me—eleven—but she's really smart. Sensei shows her a karate move one time, and Maia remembers it perfectly. Not only that, but she can teach the move to the whole class.

I don't know why, but Maia picks on me. And she's good at doing it right in the middle of class, too. Then, when I say something back to her, I'm the one who gets in trouble with Sensei. Which is why I don't like Maia very much. In karate, we're supposed to show *respect*. In my opinion, Maia could use a few lessons in *that*.

Jamie's only nine, but she seems to under-stand the dojo way of thinking the best of every-one. She tells us things her grandmother taught her. She's Native American—part Navajo and part Hopi. She wears a headband that her grandmother made for her—but she *only* wears it in the dojo. It's that special.

Anyway, even before I got into the BBC, she told me I need to learn about my Animal Power so I can learn to believe in myself. Jamie talks like a sensei sometimes. But I *do* believe in myself. . . . I believe I'm probably going to flunk out of the BBC in ten minutes!

"Good," Sensei said. "Now spread apart, and let's do some stretches."

My legs were always stiff before class. As I struggled to reach my toes, I saw that Maia was already in full splits. She gave me that 'look how good I am' smile.

After about ten minutes of toe touches, crunches, jumping jacks, and push-ups, it was time to start karate.

"Maia," called Sensei.

"*Osu*, Sensei!" yelled Maia, jumping off the floor into a fighting stance.

"I would like you to practice flip-kicks."

"*Osu*, Sensei!" she answered. She pivoted on her back foot and brought her knee front for the kick.

"Max, you will do spinning back kicks."

"*Osu*, Sensei!" I yelled. Of course I would get the kick that makes me dizzy.

"Jamie, you will do crescent kicks. Antonio, you will practice roundhouse kicks."

"*Osu*, Sensei!" they said.

I was just starting to sweat when I heard a strange chiming sound coming from the corner of the room.

"Circle time, quickly!" Sensei walked over to the chime.

We hurried into a circle and sat down as Sensei unlocked a giant oak cupboard in the corner of the dojo. She opened the door, and the music grew louder. She carefully pulled out a large wooden box and carried it to the center of the circle.

*Here is the thing that no one else gets to
see but the members of the Black Belt Club,* I
thought. *The thing that stays locked in the cupboard, and all the other kids wonder about it.*

The box was very elaborate. It was fascinat-
ing, and I studied each part of it closely. The
box looked as if it had been carved out
of a fat tree trunk. I could see pieces of bark
and knots showing from where the branches
had once been before the tree had been cut
into a box.

There were all different colors of wood on it, too, as if the box were made from every kind of tree on the planet, and unless you looked really closely, you wouldn't even notice that it had four doors. But there they were, one door carved into each side of the box, and at the very top was an acorn lid.

MAX, YOU MADE A **PROMISE** TO TRY YOUR BEST AND TO NEVER GIVE UP WHEN YOU JOINED THE BBC, REMEMBER?

WHEN YOU MAKE A PROMISE, IT'S A VERY SERIOUS COMMITMENT.

Get out! Get out now! screamed a voice in my head. But of course, being the chicken I am, I just nodded again.

"Good. Let's get started."

She held her hand over the Box of the Four Doors, opening the acorn lid. Inside was a small compartment holding five large crystals.

"Take a crystal and hold it over your head, like this." Sensei held hers high.

Just as all the crystals came together, a ray of sunlight streaked through the window, right through our stones. They glistened with the light, and rainbows lit up the room.

"Whoa!" I heard the other kids say.

The Box of the Four Doors began to spin.

"Was that music I heard?"

The box was making the sound I sometimes hear when the wind blows through the eucalyptus tree by my bedroom window. Watching the box spin was making me dizzy.

The box suddenly stopped as one of the doors flew open, and a drawer popped out. A strange glow came into focus like a 3-D picture.

Standing before us was a hologram of a little man. He wore a white turban wrapped around his head.

"Namaste," he said, and bowed with his hands in prayer position by his heart.

Maia, Antonio, and Jamie all bowed their heads. Sensei looked at me.

BUT SENSEI, I'M NOT THAT *BRAVE* OR THAT *SMART*.

IT'S ALL WAITING FOR YOU INSIDE, MAX. NOW SHOW RESPECT, PLEASE, AND BOW.

WOULD YOU TELL US ABOUT THE *TREE OF LIFE*?

THE *TREE OF LIFE* IS THE CENTER OF THE RAIN FOREST, AND FOR US, IT IS THE CENTER OF *ALL LIFE*.

THE *TREE OF LIFE* HAS THE
SEVEN WHEELS OF POWER
UPON IT.

ALL OF LIFE IS MADE OF *ENERGY*, AND IN OUR WORLD, THE SEVEN WHEELS ARE THE *CENTER OF THE ENERGY*. NOW THE POSITIVE ENERGY OF HEALTH AND LOVE ARE FADING. RESPECT AND KINDNESS ARE BEING REPLACED BY ANGER AND FEAR - WHAT WE CALL *THE DARK ENERGY*.

WHAT CAN WE DO TO *HELP?*

SOMETHING *TERRIBLE* IS HAPPENING TO THE TREE OF LIFE. **The Death Master** HAS BECOME VERY STRONG.

WHO IS THE *DEATH MASTER?*

HE IS AN *EVIL FORCE* THAT HAS COME OUT OF THE *UNDERWORLD,* AND HE WANTS THE TREE OF LIFE TO *DIE.*

WITH HIS NEW **STRENGTH**, HE HAS TAKEN THE WHEELS OFF THE TREE AND HIDDEN THEM. WITHOUT THE WHEELS, THE SACRED TREE OF LIFE WILL BE **OUT OF BALANCE** AND WILL **DIE**.

That's crazy, I thought. *Everything is going to die because a bad guy stole some wheels off a tree?* Things were sounding worse and worse. Yet I knew Sensei would never send us on a mission she thought we couldn't handle.

THESE WHEELS ARE POINTS OF **ENERGY** AND **POWER**. THEY GLOW AND SPIN AND KEEP OUR WORLD HEALTHY AND AT PEACE. BUT NOW THE ENERGY OF LIGHT IS GROWING **WEAK**. OUR WORLD IS IN DANGER OF TOTAL DESTRUCTION - **AND SO IS YOURS**.

WE DO NOT UNDERSTAND THE *REASONS* FOR THE DEATH MASTER'S ATTACK, BUT WE KNOW THAT HE MUST BE *STOPPED*.

WHY DOES HE WANT *EVERYTHING* TO DIE?

BECAUSE FOR *HIM*, THE POWER OF THE DARK IS *STRONGER* THAN THE POWER OF THE LIGHT.

WELL, IS IT?

The Sage looked around the circle at each of us. "What is day without night? We need balance. When hate becomes stronger than love, the world is out of balance. If the wheels are not returned, frightening things will happen."

The image of the Sage began to fade. "Come quickly," he said. "We have but three days left before . . . "

Then, suddenly, he disappeared.

"Three days!" I said to Sensei. "I can't be gone that long!"

Somehow I wasn't sure about that, with this Death Master guy, danger, and who knows what else. I was biting my nails again—*great*.

DO WE AT LEAST GET *WEAPONS*?

MAX, WHAT DOES THE WORD *"KARATE"* MEAN?

EMPTY HAND.

AND WHY?

BECAUSE WE LEARN HOW TO PROTECT OURSELVES *WITHOUT* WEAPONS.

KEEP THAT IN MIND. NOW, YOU MUST EACH DECIDE WHAT YOUR *PATH* WILL BE. *MAIA*, WILL YOU GO?

Maia held her crystal up to the light again, and the image of a crane shimmered inside. "In Japan, the crane symbolizes good luck and balance. I choose this power for my journey today."

Sensei looked at Antonio. He held up his
crystal. It glowed inside with the image of a bull.
"In Brazil, the bull is respected for its strong will
and power. I choose the bull. I will never give up
until the Tree of Life is safe."

Jamie held her crystal up above her head. "In honor of my Hopi and Navajo ancestors," she said, "I will see with the great vision of the eagle."

Now it was my turn. *Here goes nothing.* I held my crystal up. It began to shine, but there was nothing inside. Everyone stared at me. *Great. Of course my crystal would be empty!*

"Nothing's happening, Sensei. Maybe there's no animal for me."

"You must concentrate so your animal hears you. Now close your eyes and tell me what you see. You could try thinking of an animal from your ancestors' homeland. Sometimes our animal power has some connection to our family, but not always. Where is your family from?"

"Los Angeles. We live five blocks away."

Everyone laughed.

I closed my eyes and held on to my crystal.
I felt it warming up, but all I saw was blackness.

"Nothing's happening."

Sensei spoke softly. "Focus on the forest."

A tall pine tree came into my mind, then another, and yet another. *This is kind of cool, but where's my animal?* I kept wondering. I was following a path through a dense forest. I turned a corner, and suddenly a huge face loomed right in front of me!

"What did you see?" asked Sensei.

"A big black bear with giant teeth!" I told her, still shaken.

"That's good. That means the bear wants to share its power with you."

Or eat me alive! I thought.

SO YOU WILL WORK WITH BEAR POWER TO GAIN *STRENGTH AND COURAGE*, RIGHT?

OSU, SENSEI. DOES THIS MEAN I'LL GET A BEAR PATCH FOR THE BACK OF MY *GI*?

WE'LL SEE HOW YOU USE YOUR POWER.

WHY DID I SIGN UP FOR THIS? A BEAR. I DON'T WANT TO DIE YOUNG.

IF ONLY THERE WAS SOME WAY TO *GET OUT* OF THIS.

OKAY, BLACK BELT CLUB. TIME TO DO THE *FOUR WINDS KATA*. YOU MUST BEGIN YOUR JOURNEY NOW. EVERY MINUTE COUNTS!

We quickly stood, forming a circle.

Maia balanced as still and silent as a crane, standing on one leg. She began her kata facing East.

Antonio sank to his knees, tipping his head down. He began his kata facing South.

Jamie held her arms out wide, as if gliding like an eagle. She began her kata facing West.

And I, well—I kind of just stood there, trying to look big and mean. But I'm just regular-sized, and I'm more like a regular-sized power, not bear power.

Sensei knew I was having trouble. She was standing right next to me. "Think bear, Max," she whispered. "Focus. Go into the forest and be the bear! *Begin!*"

Then came the part I love best about karate. When I do my karate moves, I do feel strong. I had practiced the Four Winds Kata a lot since the invitation to the BBC came in the mail. I was so nervous to get it right. I knew I had to practice it over and over so my body could just remember it by itself. Sensei always tells me to just listen to my body and not think about it so much. *Here goes.*

As we all began the kata together, I could feel Sensei watching with pride. All of her students moved with ease and elegance. "I have taught them well," I heard her say softly. "Now I only hope they can win the battle ahead."

The Black Belt Club moved as one—stepping, lunging, kicking, punching, and whirling together with the movements of the Four Winds Kata. The magic of the dance was underway. Only the Black Belt Club knew this kata, and it only worked if it was performed in unison, with total focus.

"May the four winds guide you and keep you safe!" Sensei called out to us.

Suddenly, with a flash of wind and light, we were gone.

CHAPTER 3

WE WERE still dancing the Four Winds Kata when we landed in a rain forest. We were spinning, jumping, and kicking at hyperspeed and still riding the wind a little above the ground. I could feel the wet air of the rain forest all around me.

   We began to slow down. Suddenly, the wind just stopped. For a split second, we were hovering in our karate stances. But we were still up in the air!

We looked at one another, laughed, and then we fell. Everyone landed on their feet—everyone but me, of course.

Before us was a grand temple, surrounded by a lush jungle. It was all white, and it looked like the top of a wedding cake, except for one thing. Most wedding cakes don't have monsters on them!

When I tipped my head back, I could see the whole statue. It was at the base of a huge stair-case that led to a door at the top.

THAT DUDE IS *TALLER* THAN MY HOUSE!

AND *GROSS!* HE'S DRESSED LIKE A WARRIOR IN ARMOR, BUT HIS FACE LOOKS LIKE A MEAN *DOG.*

WHOA!

EARTHQUAKE!

All of us were knocked off of our feet.

"Look!" The statue had started to move!

Just as the others turned to look, the rumbling stopped, and the statue stood still.

"What?" they asked.

IT MOVED! THAT *MONSTER STATUE* MOVED! LET'S JUST DO OUR KATA NOW AND *GET BACK* TO THE DOJO!

Antonio stepped closer to the statue. "No way! We have a mission to do. Look, I'll show you. Don't be such a chicken." He walked over to the statue and poked it with his finger.

SEE? JUST A PIECE OF *ROCK.*

The statue stayed frozen in place.

Suddenly, the statue's arm shot straight out and grabbed Antonio. He struggled to get free, but the monster lifted him high into the air.

I yelled. The monster slashed at us with his huge fist. I jumped aside and barely escaped. "We're under attack!"

Swoosh! The statue slashed left and right and up and down. Antonio was in the air, trying to kick his feet. He was pushing hard, but he couldn't hurt the monster.

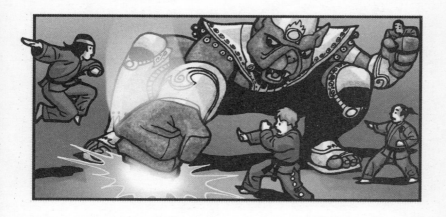

SPLIT UP! DEFEND IN CIRCLE FORMATION!

Jamie circled around and started running at the monster at full speed. She skipped into a cartwheel and sprang into the air. With a twisting flip, she landed on the monster's neck. He flailed at her, but Jamie dodged him with the swiftness of her eagle.

She signaled to me again, and I shrugged.

OH GREAT! IT FIGURES *YOU* WOULDN'T KNOW THE *SECRET* BLACK BELT CLUB *HAND SIGNAL CODE!*

OKAY, HERE'S THE PLAN. WHEN I GIVE YOU *THIS* SIGNAL, YOU DO A *SPINNING REVERSE WHEEL KICK* ON HIS LEFT LEG WHILE I DO ONE ON HIS RIGHT.

Okay, I can do this. This is the part I like— *the karate part.*

Quickly, she gave me the sign for the double sweep.

I stepped forward with my left foot and spun quickly around, letting my leg whip in a circle with the speed of a baseball bat and—I was hoping—the power of a bear. It was perfect! Right on target! But the monster saw us coming.

He merely lifted his foot, avoiding our sweep.

Antonio was still captive, and we had already used our best karate moves! *What now?*

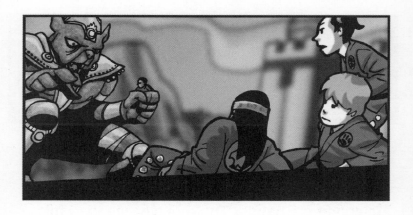

Just then, the monster threw Antonio straight at us. He flew like a bowling ball and made a strike as all three of us tumbled to the ground in a pile.

Antonio gagged and coughed. Then the monster shook like a dog and threw Jamie off.

This is it, my mind flashed. *I'm chopped liver. What a way to die!*

Just as the monster was coming at us, the Sage appeared at the top of the staircase and clapped his hands. The monster stopped mid-swing. Slowly and precisely, he took three steps backward, returning to his position at the base of the stairs.

Once again, he was just a statue.

"Thank you!" We stood up and bowed.

"Come up here. I have things to show you."

Keeping an eye on the monster, we cautiously climbed the steps. As I walked past him, I thought I saw his arm begin to move. I ran.

At the top of the stairs, we all looked with amazement into a huge, cavernous space.

LOOK, YOGA!

WE DO YOGA IN *KARATE* TO STRETCH OUR MUSCLES.

THAT IS VERY GOOD, INDEED. PEOPLE HAVE BEEN DOING YOGA FOR THOUSANDS OF YEARS. IT IS A VERY *ANCIENT ART.*

LOOK AT THAT MAN OVER THERE WITH HIS FOOT BEHIND HIS NECK! HE LOOKS LIKE A *PRETZEL.*

OOOHHHMMM.

WHAT'S WRONG WITH THEM?

THERE'S NOTHING WRONG WITH THEM. IT'S A *SPECIAL MEDITATION SOUND.*

BUT WHY?

BE OBSERVANT. LOOK AROUND THE ROOM. SEE IF YOU CAN FIGURE IT OUT.

It was impossible to miss another giant stone statue. Luckily, this guy looked a lot nicer. He was bald and sat with his legs crisscrossed. His eyes were closed, and seven different colored lights beamed from his body.

Most of the meditating people were sitting the same way. And every time they made that *om* sound, the colors on the statue glowed brighter.

When the *om* sound stopped, the colors dimmed.

I turned to the Sage. "Doing yoga with that *om* sound makes the lights shine brighter, right?"

He smiled. "The lights are what we call the seven energy points on the body. Doing exercises like yoga and karate makes these energy points healthy and in balance. If you keep your energy healthy, your body will stay healthy. And," he added, "you must stay healthy to be powerful."

Just then, the ground started rumbling again. It sounded like the monster's rumble!

Roar! Rumble! Roar!

A huge Bengal tiger leaped through the window and into the temple. Riding on its back was a man with an angry, pinched face. His cloak was dark.

My legs began shaking. I jumped up into fighting stance. *This is the bad guy*, I thought. I could feel it all through my body.

The man and the tiger stood next to the statue guy, but instead of glowing brighter, the lights went out! Then the man looked at the Sage and let out a nasty laugh.

Maia jumped into a fighting stance, ready for action if needed.

"She has the best technique of all of us. She'll get him," Jamie whispered.

Antonio was watching Maia, too, and he yelled at the tiger man, hoping to distract him. "Hey, puke breath! Maybe you don't know who we are?"

"I know who you are, little boy."

Maia suddenly jumped at him with a flying side kick. She had perfect aim and speed.

He raised his hand in defense and created some kind of force field that stopped Maia in midair!

Then, he raised his hand and sent her flying backwards. We jumped out of the way—just in time. She landed at our feet.

The room grew darker.

YOUR *LITTLE* BLACK BELT CLUB DOESN'T HAVE A CHANCE. IN THREE DAYS, THE TREE OF LIFE BECOMES THE *TREE OF DEATH*! ENJOY YOUR LAST DAYS ON A GREEN PLANET, BECAUSE SOON IT WILL BE MY FAVORITE COLOR: *BLACK*!

The tiger roared, giving us a nice view of its jagged teeth. Then, they leaped out the window, taking the darkness with them.

OKAY, I GIVE UP. *WHO* WAS THAT?

THAT, MY FRIENDS, WAS THE *DEATH MASTER* - KNOWN TO US AS Master Mundi.

I DON'T GET IT. HOW IS HE GOING TO BRING DEATH TO EVERYTHING?

HE'S MAKING DEATH INTO A *GAME*. HE HAS THE SEVEN WHEELS OF POWER, AND HE'S *HIDDEN* THEM.

SO WE'LL GO *FIND* THEM.

ARE YOU OKAY?

EVIL ENERGY MAKES ME TIRED.

MY GRANDMOTHER IS A *MEDICINE WOMAN*. AND SHE TAUGHT ME HOW TO *PROTECT* MYSELF FROM EVIL ENERGY.

WHAT ARE YOU TALKING ABOUT?

TO PROTECT MYSELF FROM EVIL, I NEED TO PUT AN INDIVIDUAL BALL OF *LIGHT* AROUND MYSELF - LIKE AN INVISIBLE *FORCE FIELD*. THEN NO ONE CAN STEAL MY ENERGY.

YES, WE DO THAT HERE, TOO, BY *MEDITATING*. TODAY MASTER MUNDI CAUGHT ME BY SURPRISE. HE'S NEVER BEEN ABLE TO GET INTO THIS TEMPLE BEFORE. OUR POWERS SEEM TO BE GROWING *WEAKER*.

WELL, IF YOUR POWERS CAN'T PROTECT YOU, THEN HOW ARE WE SUPPOSED TO?

I DON'T KNOW HOW HE GOT IN. MAYBE WE ARE WEAKENED BECAUSE HE IS KILLING THE TREE OF LIFE?

IT'S A DANGEROUS JOURNEY. YOU HAVE JUST BEEN WARNED. YOU MUST EACH DECIDE IF YOU ARE WILLING TO CONTINUE.

SO WHAT'S OUR PLAN? IF WE ONLY HAVE THREE DAYS, WE NEED A PLAN!

OKAY, THEN, MY DECISION IS TO GET OUT OF HERE. I MEAN, DID YOU GUYS SEE THE *SIZE* OF THAT TIGER? MAYBE THIS IS A GOOD TIME TO HEAD BACK *HOME*. YOU KNOW: BOOKS, TELEVISION, A WARM BED....

AND PIZZA. AND *MOMMY*, TO TUCK HER LITTLE *BABY* INTO BED.

MY *MOTHER* IS GONE! WHY DON'T YOU *SHUT UP!*

I chewed on my lip. I was afraid to stay, but I was even more afraid to quit. *Try your best*, I seemed to hear Sensei whisper. "Okay! I'm in!"

We gave each other high fives. Maia missed my hand on purpose, but the decision to stay felt like a good one.

WISE CHOICE. YOU SEE, MY FRIENDS, THE TREE OF LIFE AFFECTS US ALL, NOT JUST THIS FOREST. FOLLOW ME.

We faced the statue and saw that a scroll rested in its upturned hands. The Sage took the scroll down and unrolled it.

I hope it's a map, I thought, *because with all the weird, crawly things that live in the rain forest, I want to know where to step and where not to step.*

When the scroll was unrolled, it was almost as long as the Sage was tall. But instead of paper, it was made out of clear fabric. Something was moving on it. And it sure seemed to be a map—and a tree.

"What kind of map is this?" I asked, and I took a big step back, just in case.

The picture on the fabric appeared to be moving—as if a breeze was in the room.

There were gold leaves, silver leaves, red, white, and yellow leaves. There were even purple ones. The bark was all different colors, too: white, brown, gray, orange, and mustard.

Antonio touched the clear fabric, and it shivered. "Weird. But where's the map?"

"You must follow the clues." The Sage opened another clear scroll and placed it on top of the first one. There they were: the Seven Wheels of Power!

"It's beautiful!" exclaimed Jamie. The Seven Wheels were all spinning in a straight line. They were in exactly the same order as the colors of the rainbow. Red was at the bottom of the trunk. Just above red was orange. Then yellow, green, blue, and indigo. Last was violet, at the very top of the tree.

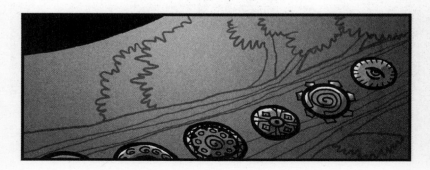

"The wheels are the energy centers," the Sage explained. "Look closely."

When I looked more carefully, I saw that beside the wheels were bright reflections of animals.

Next to the red and orange wheels, the image of a bull shimmered.

We each began looking for our animal power on the Tree.

"Look! Yellow and green must be my wheels of power because the crane is standing right next to them!" Maia said.

"Excellent," said the Sage.

Antonio looked at me. "She's good."

Jamie touched the blue wheel on the scroll. "The eagle pierces the bright blue sky!" said Jamie. "I'll find the blue wheel!"

"So I guess this leaves that bluish-purplish color for me?"

Maia rolled her eyes.

DUH, MAX – IT IS THE ONE WITH THE *BEAR* NEXT TO IT.

WHAT ABOUT THE *TOP WHEEL*? WHY ISN'T THERE AN ANIMAL NEXT TO THAT ONE?

THAT IS THE *DREAM WHEEL*. IT HOLDS THE ENERGY OF OUR *IMAGINATION*, *HOPES*, AND *DREAMS*. AND NOW, YOU MUST REMEMBER WHAT I SAY.

THE LONGEST NIGHT OF THE YEAR APPROACHES. THE WHEELS MUST BE *RETURNED* TO THE TREE OF LIFE BEFORE THAT NIGHT ARRIVES. YOU MUST *FIND* THEM. YOU ARE OUR LAST CHANCE - OR *EVERYTHING* ON THE PLANET WILL DIE.

EVEN US?

WE ARE ALL *ONE*. WE ARE ALL CONNECTED.

IS THAT A YES?

THAT IS A *YES*, INDEED.

CHAPTER 4

I LOOKED back at the Sage as we headed down the trail into the forest. I could hear him repeating something over and over.

"What's he doing?" I asked Maia.

"He's chanting."

"What's the point of chanting?"

"It's like saying a prayer. Now be quiet!" she said as if I were the most annoying pest in the world.

Somehow his chanting didn't make me feel any better.

He had given each of us a pack with some food, water, sandals, and camping gear in it. He'd said we only needed enough for three days because that was all the time we had to save the Tree. And if we didn't save the Tree in three days, nothing would matter anyway. Not a very good pep talk, if you ask me. He also gave us some rope, matches to light a fire, blankets, and two machetes. He said we'd need them to cut away the thick vines along the trail.

Maia and Antonio grabbed the machetes first. I noticed they always liked being the leaders, even though Maia and I are actually the oldest. Jamie likes to *think* about being the leader, and I . . . well . . . I don't ever *want* to be the leader. If I were the leader, probably nobody would listen to me anyway.

We all followed Maia as the jungle grew thicker and thicker. Luckily, the Sage had also given us the map—if you could call it that. What we really had was a picture of the Tree of Life with the Seven Wheels, and a big jungle ahead of us.

STAY IN A *STRAIGHT LINE!* THIS PATH'S NOT VERY WIDE.

After a minute, we started walking again, this time more quietly. There it was again. We stopped. It stopped. Whatever *it* was, it was moving when we were moving.

The branches were already getting thicker across the trail, and Maia and Antonio had started chopping them with the machetes.

Suddenly, the huge Bengal tiger from the temple jumped out in front of us on the trail. It roared and flashed its teeth.

"Watch out!" I yelled. But I was too late.

The tiger pounced on Maia and Antonio, but Maia managed a sword-hand strike, hitting its paw away. Antonio followed with a hammerfist strike to its nose. It pulled back with a roar.

Jamie screamed. It turned to leap at her. I jumped into action with a spinning back kick. I got it! The tiger fell sideways with a moan.

Suddenly, something fell on us from above.

"What's happening?" I yelled.

Dark, creepy vines whipped around us, entangling our arms and legs. In seconds, we dangled helplessly above the ground. The tiger crouched, ready for a final pounce.

A sinister laugh made my heart skip a beat.
It was the Death Master—Master Mundi.

Maia struggled and kicked.

I squirmed to get free, but it wasn't working. I heard another rustling noise behind me again. I tried to see what it was, but I couldn't move. Maia was tangled up in front of me.

Just then, one of the vines around my arms loosened.

DID YOU *FEEL* THAT?

YEAH, I CAN ALMOST GET MY ARM FREE!

WHAT'S GOING ON UP THERE?

WOULDN'T *YOU* LIKE TO KNOW!

MY GOODNESS, AREN'T WE *DEFIANT*?

WHAT DO YOU KNOW ABOUT *GOODNESS*?

Oh, great, I thought. I am going to be cat food. I have a cat, and I've seen how they eat— one morsel at a time, chewing each piece really well.

"You kids don't have any plans, do you?" Master Mundi asked.

And then, like a flash, he disappeared.

All of us were wiggling desperately to get untangled.

HEY, STOP *FIGHTING!* WE HAVE TO WORK TOGETHER, RIGHT?

YEAH, REMEMBER WHAT THE SAGE SAID? *"WE ARE ALL ONE!"*

THAT'S JUST NOT POSSIBLE.

LOOK! THE *MACHETES* ARE ON THE GROUND BELOW US.

SHHH! THERE IT IS AGAIN - LISTEN.

The rustling noise grew louder and louder. Nervous, we looked around in all directions.

What was making the noise? Suddenly, two of the vines snapped. We dropped with a lurch and dangled halfway to the ground.

"Whoa! What happened?" I yelled.

We clung together for dear life. The rustling noise continued, but I still couldn't see anything.

We fell straight to the ground. Luckily, the ground in the rain forest was pretty soft. As I lay there, I looked at it more closely. Something was moving, busy under the leaves.

Two long tentacles popped out at my face. "Outdoor life is not for me!" I said, jumping up quickly.

LOOK, IT'S A RAT *CHEWING* ON THE VINES!

SO THAT WAS THE RUSTLING NOISE WE KEPT HEARING. THE RAT MUST HAVE SET US FREE. BUT WHY WOULD A RAT HELP US?

I DON'T KNOW, AND I DON'T THINK I WANT TO FIND OUT.

GOING SO SOON?

I turned to see the Sage.

Suddenly, the rat scurried down the tree and ran to him.

The rat disappeared into the Sage's robes. Then he popped his head out and wiggled his whiskers.

MY RAT IS SMALL, BUT VERY *SMART*.

BECAUSE OF HIM, YOU WERE ALL *FREED*.

REMEMBER THAT EVEN THE SMALLEST CREATURES HAVE *GREAT POWER* IF THEY KNOW HOW TO USE THEM.

WE GIVE YOU MANY *THANKS*.

The Sage stood up and started to leave.

I didn't know what to say.

I took a step toward him.

"But wait!" I exclaimed. "Where are you going?"

And then, he was gone.

CHAPTER 5

DEATH WAS everywhere. We were on the trail, and I had the feeling that the Tree was near. Dead plants were all around us, dried up as if the life had been sucked right out of them. It was definitely spooky.

"Keep an eye out for Master Mundi," warned Maia.

"I keep getting the feeling that we're being watched," I whispered.

The trail looked as if it had turned into dark, flowing liquid. It was headed straight for us.

We jumped and rolled off the trail, just in time, as millions and billions of huge ants poured by us like a rushing river.

We scurried alongside the ants, going upriver, and then we turned the corner. All of us stopped in our tracks, utterly amazed.

There it was. The most magnificent tree on the entire planet stood before our very eyes. A tree like no other—gigantic, perfectly formed, and brilliantly colored.

Its branches extended as far as the eye could see. *And it was being eaten alive.* The great Tree of Life was covered with millions of leaf-cutter ants. My jaw was stuck wide open in shock.

WE'VE GOT TO DO *SOMETHING!*

THAT TREE WON'T LAST FOR THREE MORE DAYS, EVEN IF WE DO FIND THE WHEELS!

I THINK YOU'RE *RIGHT.*

As we watched, the stream of ants dropped their leaves and turned to face us.

UH, HEY GUYS...

WHAT KIND OF *KARATE MOVES* WORK ON ANTS?

But it was too late. The ants were upon us, swarming our bodies.

I tried my best moves. I spun around and around to throw them off of me, but their feet were sticky. Then I tried some front shoulder rolls and break falls. I managed to toss off a few, but they just kept coming.

We were all rolling on the ground trying to squash them when they began biting us.

Yeah, right. Make it rain? I thought. But I guess the others thought they could, because they began yelling at the clouds.

If this works, I thought, *I'll believe anything.*

It wasn't looking good. Red bite marks swelled up all over my skin. *I hope I'm not allergic to these ants*, I thought, *because I am allergic to so many things*. I kicked and jabbed. Four enormous ants fell to the ground.

The few drops on my face quickly turned into a rainstorm. Then, it began to pour, and pour, and pour. The ants ran for cover, many of them burrowing into the soft, moist ground.

In the meantime, we were getting soaked.

"What's that rushing sound?" I asked, look-ing around.

"It's probably that river I saw over there," Antonio said, pointing to the west.

"But it's coming from that way!" I said, pointing in the opposite direction.

We took off and made it to the trees just as the water swept by us. It was sucking up everything in its path, including thousands of ants. But the new river that cut through the forest separated us from the Tree of Life.

Maia scouted a path through the trees.

"Monkey power!" I joked, but nobody laughed.

As we reached the trees, Maia grabbed a vine and swung to a branch.

Jamie reached up to swing next. Suddenly, her hand slipped, and she lost her grip. "Ahhh!"

Maia grabbed her arm just in time, pulling her to safety. Jamie was shaking.

I grabbed a vine and took a leap of faith.

I made a huge swing and landed ahead of
everyone else.

LET'S HAVE A *RACE*.
FIRST ONE ACROSS WINS...

...THE FIRST *PUNCH* ON
MASTER MUNDI!

With confidence, Antonio grabbed a vine
and swung—ahead of me.

That's not what I had in mind, I thought, but
all of us took off swinging to the challenge.

Maia swung ahead, into the lead.

Sure, I thought. And of course everyone made it across before me. Well, I was kind of used to that. I ran to catch up.

Everyone stood before the Tree of Life. Again, we stared in wonder at its majesty.

"Ahhh!" Jamie and I cried, startled. The Death Master, Master Mundi, had appeared out of nowhere and stood right beside us.

I HAVE TAKEN *SIX* OF THE WHEELS OFF THE TREE OF LIFE. I HAVE *HIDDEN* THEM IN DIFFERENT PARTS OF THE FOREST. IN ORDER TO WIN THE GAME, YOU MUST FIND THE SIX WHEELS AND PLACE THEM BACK ON THE TREE, IN THE *RIGHT ORDER*, BY MIDNIGHT, TWO DAYS FROM NOW.

BUT THE SAGE SAID WE HAD *THREE* DAYS.

THAT OLD *FOOL!* THIS IS MY GAME, AND I MAKE THE RULES. SINCE YOU SPOILED MY ANTS' *TEA PARTY*, YOU HAVE TO PAY THE PRICE. THE GREAT *TREE OF LIFE* WILL SOON BECOME THE EVEN GREATER *TREE OF DEATH*. AND THEN, KITTY GETS TO *EAT!*

The tiger roared, and they slunk away.

CHAPTER 6

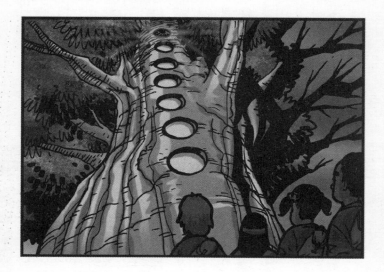

THE GLORIOUS Tree of Life stood before us. Six round openings had been carved into the trunk of the Tree.

"Those openings must be where the six wheels fit into the Tree," said Maia. "Look! The seventh wheel is still on top."

At the top of the tree I saw the Dream Wheel, still in place. "Why didn't he hide that one?"

DON'T YOU EVER LISTEN? THE SAGE TOLD US THAT THE *DREAMTIME WHEEL* STAYS ON TOP.

IT MUST BE TOO *POWERFUL* TO STEAL - EVEN FOR THE DEATH MASTER. BUT IF THE OTHER WHEELS ARE NOT *RETURNED*, THEN THE TREE WILL DIE, RIGHT?

NOT IF *WE* CAN HELP IT.

SO WHERE ARE THEY? I MEAN, THIS IS A *HUGE FOREST*. HOW DO WE KNOW WHERE TO LOOK?

"Remember the temple! We have to think about the clues!" said Maia.

Antonio shook his head. "This is a stupid game, and this Mundi guy is evil. I say we figure out how to trap him, use our karate moves on him, and make him put the wheels back himself!"

I was hoping I sounded smart, but I don't think I fooled anyone. They all knew I didn't like sparring in class, so why would I like real fighting? My stomach was growling again. "Hey, when do we eat, anyway?"

I took a step backward. What was going on?
"Hey, you guys," I began. But before I could say
any more, they all lunged at me!

I barely missed getting knocked over by a hopping front kick from Antonio.

Jamie tried to sweep me and threw a back knuckle strike toward my head. I blocked it just in time.

Then Maia did a quick spinning back kick. I countered with a reverse punch right into her stomach. She coughed and fell to the ground.

I had knocked the wind out of her, but that didn't stop the other guys. They were still attacking. Maia coughed again and shook her head as if she were waking up.

Antonio let me go. All of them shook their heads as if coming out of a haze.

"What just happened?" asked Antonio. "I'm sorry, Max. I don't know what happened. All I could think about was beating you up!"

"Me, too!" said Maia. "That was really weird."

"I think we'd better stop and focus. Let's concentrate on our Animal Powers," said Jamie.

"Sounds good to me," I said, rubbing my sore arms.

We took our crystals out of our packs and stood in a circle. Then we held our crystals up to the sky to catch a ray of light. But the sky was filling up with dark clouds.

"Now what?" I asked. "We need a beam of sunlight to activate our Animal Powers."

I looked up at the gathering clouds, and I thought I heard Mundi's laugh, riding on the wind. I got goose bumps.

THIS IS NOT GOOD. WE NEED HELP, AND THE DARKNESS IS GROWING *STRONGER*.

I looked up at the Tree of Life. A glimmer of light reflected off a large, silver leaf near the seventh wheel. For some reason, the leaf hadn't been touched by the ants. Maybe the light on the leaf would shine down on our crystals.

LOOK UP *THERE!*

THE TREE IS TRYING TO HELP US. IT'S TRYING TO SHINE SOME *LIGHT* OUR WAY.

IF WE HOLD THE CRYSTALS A LITTLE HIGHER, WE CAN CATCH THE RAY!

We stood on our tiptoes, reaching up and holding our crystals to the sky.

"We got it!" I called as the light shot through our four crystals all at once.

The white light split into seven different-colored lights. The colors shone on each one of us.

I looked at Antonio. He was bathed in red and orange light, and he began stomping his feet like a bull. He looked as if he were ready to charge.

Maia was all yellow and green, and it gave her an eerie glow. She stood gracefully on one leg like a crane.

That's good, I thought. *Everybody's saying such cool things. What am I going to say? I'll probably sound like a dork.*

Jamie was bathed in cool, blue light. She opened her arms wide.

Now everyone looked at me. I was glowing, too. *The color is kind of weird. It's like a dark, bluish purple. My turn. But what to say?*

What am I saying? That was so lame. My stomach growled again. Or was it my stomach? I heard the growl again, but it wasn't because I was hungry. The sound was coming from deep inside me! I felt wider, bigger, more powerful. Then I realized I was feeling big and fierce and strong. *What is this?*

We all lifted our crystals high again and called out, "Four Winds!"

Suddenly, I could feel my Animal Power.

The sky grew darker as thunder and lightning crashed around us.

"Let's go," said Maia. "This storm makes me think that Master Mundi must feel our Animal Powers. We'll have to split up to distract him. Besides, the wheels are probably hidden in different parts of the forest. Good luck, everyone—and let your animal guide you!"

I looked up from my thoughts, and I was alone. The sky was definitely getting darker. Doom and gloom were everywhere. I walked in the direction of the Tree of Life, and something caught my eye. On the ground lay the large silver leaf that had reflected the light for our Animal Powers.

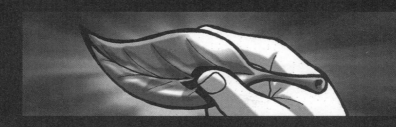

I picked it up carefully. It was the most beautiful leaf I had ever seen. I put it in my pack and scanned the four directions. Which way now? I smelled something coming. Bears have a powerful sense of smell, I realized. I know bears can smell things from far away. My bear power was definitely kicking in because—ugh! Something smelled horrible. Then I recognized the scent: Puja!

CHAPTER 7

I WAS heading north—into bear country. I hoped I was leaving Puja far behind. I wandered through pine trees, up a mountainside, and over to the cliffs.

"A cave. Yes!" Of course, that's where bears hibernate. My wheel must be in there! I squeezed through the small opening. The cave was dark, but I could see quartz crystals on the walls.

This is so cool! But then I heard a noise and stopped. *Wait a minute. What am I doing? This is a real cave, where real bears live!*

The light went out in the cave. I turned to the opening and saw a huge, shadowy shape in front of it, blocking out the light. *Oh, no! I'm right, and I'm dead meat.*

The shape moved into the cave, letting in more light. I backed up slowly, but I was freaking out, wondering what to do. Suddenly, the shape came closer. Then it roared! The sound echoed off the cave walls, and I almost had to cover my ears. *That doesn't sound like a bear*, I thought. Then a sliver of light reflected off a gleaming pair of eyes. It was just enough to recognize . . .

The huge cat scratched at the earth and was about to leap. *This is it. It's now or never.* If I don't use my Animal Power, then why do I have it?

I stood as tall as I could and raised my hands high, like claws. *Here goes nothing.* I opened my mouth and let out the loudest bear growl I could muster.

The whole cave shook! Puja's eyes grew wide with fear, and she backed out of the cave, scared! Then she ran away.

Wow! It worked! And I actually sounded like a real bear. I do have bear power! Awesome!

My arms were still in the air. I let out another bear call, just to feel the power one more time, but my voice sounded completely normal.

"Hey, what happened?" I said aloud. I tried growling again. And again. All I heard was my same old voice. What was going on?

And then the cave began to shake again with a huge bear growl—but it wasn't coming from me.

I turned around slowly. Right behind me stood a huge black bear, standing tall on its hind legs. We were face-to-face! We both roared again as I jumped into fighting stance. *Karate won't work on a bear*, I thought, terrified. *I'm dead, I'm dead, I'm . . .*

Think quick, think quick, I thought. I pulled the crystal out of my pack. The light from the opening of the cave shone through it, and the bear image inside the crystal lit up. The real bear saw it and stopped. It looked at the crystal, and then it looked at me.

I stayed in my fighting stance, not sure what was going to happen next. Then my crystal started doing something strange. It glowed bright, then dim, then bright, then dim—as if the battery were going out. Then, all of a sudden, the crystals on the wall of the cave began blinking the same way.

The bear gave out a low growl and sat down.

I heard a voice in my mind say, *Bears like to be alone, but since you have the power, you can stay.*

I looked at the bear, and I think he smiled at me. *Maybe he's trying to get me off guard before he mauls me or eats me,* I thought.

DON'T WORRY. I ATE ALREADY.

IS IT YOUR *VOICE* I'M HEARING?

RELAX.

JUST FOCUS AND DIRECT YOUR *THOUGHTS* TOWARD ME, AND I'LL HEAR YOU.

DOES THAT MEAN YOU'RE NOT GOING TO *EAT* ME?

The bear opened his mouth and gave a big yawn. His teeth glistened.

We have work to do. Let's begin. He lay down and closed his eyes.

Better a nap than mealtime, I thought as I stepped quietly backward toward the opening of the cave.

I was starting to sweat. *Oh, I get it*, I thought. *As soon as I close my eyes, I'm easy prey. One bite, and my head disappears.*

IF I WANTED TO *EAT* YOU, I WOULD HAVE DONE IT BY NOW. YOU NEED TO HELP YOUR FRIENDS FIND THEIR *WHEELS OF POWER*, DON'T YOU?

HOW DID *YOU* KNOW?

I SEE MANY THINGS, *BROTHER BEAR.* AND NOW IT'S TIME FOR YOU TO STEP INTO YOUR *POWER* AS WELL.

BUT I HAVEN'T *FOUND* MY WHEEL YET.

THEN WHAT'S *THAT?*

On the ceiling of the cave was a big wheel, larger than a plate, with purple crystals around the edge.

Use your power, he said.

I followed him outside the cave. Somehow, from the mountainside, I could see the entire forest at once. I saw the parts that were dead and the parts that were still green and alive.

I focused my mind again and saw that in every direction my friends were in trouble.

Antonio was in the south, sinking in some reddish-brown quicksand. He was holding his red and orange wheels high above his head so they wouldn't sink with him. *Where is his bull? I don't see it. There it is! Oh, no!* Its horns were tangled up in a pile of dead branches.

I saw a spark of light out of the corner of my eye. Fire! Fire was burning through the dead brush all around him and was getting closer and closer to Antonio!

"Rats!" I yelled. *Rats? Wait a minute. . . . What about the Sage? He said we had the power within us to save ourselves if we were in danger. But how do I do that?*

As I started to concentrate, I spotted Maia in the east. A swirling, yellow wind had trapped her inside a circle. Every time she tried to escape, she was blown down to the ground.

She was holding the yellow and green wheels close to her body. Her crane was trying to help her, but the wind was too strong.

Jamie was in the dark and stormy waters of the west. The water was bubbling violently. It was trying to pull her under!

Jamie's wheel was blue. Her eagle held the wheel in its beak, trying to keep it safe from the dangerous whirlpool.

Her eagle was trying to grab her with its talons, but the stormy water splashed her eagle away each time it came close.

Everyone needs help right now, all at the same time! What can I do?

My heart was racing. Suddenly, I could feel a new power, surging inside me. It was as if the entire universe was humming—all together and in perfect harmony. It was a strange but wonderful feeling.

I took a deep breath and looked again at my friends in trouble. It was time for me to let go of my fear and have faith in myself. I yelled to my friends as loud as I could.

Antonio seemed to hear me. Instead of fighting the thick mud, he churned his body as he would for a spin kick. It helped him! He spun over to the branch and escaped the grip of the quicksand.

Maia and Jamie threw their arms apart. Yes!
They were doing it, too!

They whipped their arms and legs in a circle
motion and began to spin. By connecting to the
spiral current of the water and wind, they set
themselves free!

Suddenly, something knocked me hard. Ah! I tumbled down the mountain. I finally stopped rolling at the base of the Tree of Life. When I looked up, something was hovering over me.

He thrust his hand at my face! I did a quick side-roll up onto one knee and did a mule kick to the side of his leg. Master Mundi was down!

A frightening death-roar broke my moment of glory. Puja leaped at me!

Pow! Antonio tried to scare the tiger with a flying side kick. Puja ran to Master Mundi's side. Now they were a team.

"Max!" yelled Jamie and Maia. They dashed to me with their glowing wheels held high. As they got closer, Puja backed up.

LOOK!

THE *COMBINED* POWER OF THE WHEELS IS TOO *STRONG* FOR THEM.

MASTER MUNDI! YOU *CANNOT* WIN YOUR FIGHT AGAINST THE *POWERS OF THE LIGHT!*

I WILL NOT *RUN* FROM YOU, YOU MEANINGLESS, SIMPLE BEINGS! YOU HAVE NO IDEA WHO *I AM*. I AM THE ONE WHO KNOWS THE *SECRET OF LIFE* IN THIS WORLD!

I THOUGHT YOU WERE THE *SECRET OF DEATH*, MR. DEATH MASTER.

Master Mundi jumped onto Puja. They stalked toward us. With a heart-stopping roar, the tiger leaped in the air. Without a word, the four of us sidestepped into our directions of power. As Puja landed, I threw a pivoting side kick.

Maia did a perfect jumping front heel kick. "We got him, Max! Good job!" Puja ran.

Antonio screamed, *"Kiai!"* at the top of his lungs. He double-stepped to the right and did a spinning reverse wheel kick. Master Mundi jumped off his tiger and suddenly lunged at Jamie.

Then I understood. We needed to get the wheels onto the tree so the balance of light would return. It was the only way to defeat him.

For a split second, we all looked at one another. It was a look of power. We knew we were the Black Belt Club!

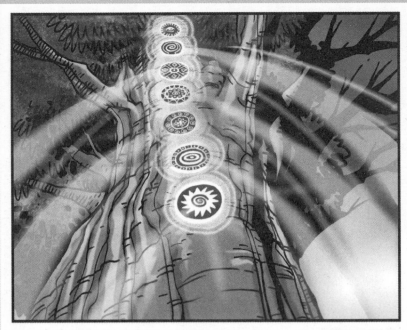

THE POWER OF THE LIGHT *WINS!*

NO! NO!

YES! YES!

The wheels had connected with the tree. The dream wheel had been very dim. Now it was ablaze. All the wheels lit up like seven suns.

NOTHING EVER DIES, LITTLE BOY. IT JUST CHANGES. THE POWER OF THE DARK ENERGY MOVES THROUGH ME, AND IT'S TIME IT MOVED THROUGH YOU, TOO!

Master Mundi lunged at me. My neck was almost in his grasp when suddenly the Tree of Life quivered. Mundi stopped in his tracks and turned to the tree. Seven rainbow-colored beams of light shot through his body, all at once. His form began to break apart. He spun so fast he spiraled up like a dark cylinder.

He became a tornado of death, sucking us
to him! We grabbed one another.

Suddenly, the cyclone stopped.

The sage smiled. "You have managed to restore the balance of light and dark in only one day. You truly understand the power of teamwork."

"Thank you, Sage." We bowed to him.

I like this, I thought. *This feels good. For the first time in my life, I feel amazingly happy. I could get used to this Black Belt Club.*

All six wheels, plus the seventh Dream Wheel, were now lined up on the tree. The tree was glowing and growing new leaves by the second. Everywhere we looked, the forest began blooming again. We stood in a circle with our animals close to us.

We pulled our crystals out and held them up together. As the light shimmered through our stones, our animals slowly disappeared. I felt my bear power deep within me as I began doing the Four Winds Kata. I moved like a bear, feeling its strength and courage. We circled and stepped, each moving like our animals. We balanced and kicked. We lunged and punched. We danced a powerful kata, first slowly, then faster and faster and faster until we finally broke through time in a flash of wind and light.

CHAPTER 8

"VERY GOOD!" said Sensei. "The Four Winds Kata looks better every time I see it. Champions of the Four Winds, that was a great workout today. Class is over. Let's line up."

I looked at her, confused.

"What do you mean, Sensei?" I asked, bewildered. "We have to tell you about the special mission we just completed. It was scary and dangerous, but I, um, well, I was the one who really saved the Tree of Life."

The other kids were silent. They just stared at me.

We bowed and shook hands good-bye. I put on my shoes and grabbed my pack. I watched through the glass doors as the next class entered the dojo and began doing stretches, getting ready for their workout.

I was digging inside my pack for the paper
when I felt something odd. I gently pulled it out.
It was a silver leaf from the Tree of Life!

BUT I WAS A **HERO** TODAY! I REALLY WAS, AND...

I DON'T HAVE TIME FOR YOUR **FAIRY TALES**, MAX. I'LL BE IN THE CAR. **HURRY UP!**

I looked across the dojo at Sensei. She stood tall and gave me a warm smile. I held up the leaf, and she winked at me.

**Turn the page for more
about karate!**

BASIC KARATE TECHNIQUES

When Max Greene was training for his black belt, he practiced these karate moves. Be sure an adult is present to help you. And remember: The karate you learn here is only used for self-defense, and only when there is no other option.

basic stance **horse stance** **ready stance**

upward block

x-block

inward block

downward block

front kick

side kick

back kick

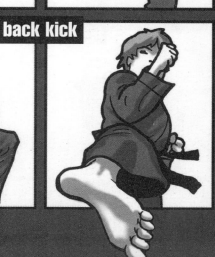

straight punch

palmheel strike

hammerfist strike

roundhouse kick

wheel kick

ABOUT THIS BOOK

KARATE IS a type of martial art where a student learns physical and mental discipline for balance of mind, body, and spirit. The power of karate can be used for harm or for healing; it is up to the individual as to which path he/she chooses to take. It is believed that martial arts were created several thousand years ago in China by Shaolin monks who needed a way to protect themselves from traveling warlords. Over time, martial arts evolved into hundreds of different styles that spread throughout the East, including Japan. The karate practiced by the Black Belt Club is based upon a traditional style from Japan called Shotokan. Shotokan karate was created by Gichin Funakoshi as a combat art for the military about one hundred years ago. The word karate means "empty hand" because we learn how to protect ourselves without using weapons. Some of the advanced spinning techniques that the BBC uses in this book come from other styles.

Today, we study karate not as a way to hurt someone, but as a way to gain confidence, focus, and fitness. When you begin to study karate, you will practice your basic techniques in a dojo. Dojo means "the place of the way"—the way of discipline in mind, body, and spirit. You will wear a uniform called a *gi*, with a white belt. If you practice regularly, over the course of four to six years you will graduate through different colored belts until you reach black belt. During your karate practice, you will learn about pressure points on the body that are soft and when hit can stop an attacker from hurting you. You will learn about meditation—a time when you can calm your mind to focus. Some teachers may even show you how to meditate on animal powers for extra strength with your karate moves. The philosophy of martial arts has been passed down through the centuries by many masters. Though karate styles may vary, all masters can agree on one important principle: Every day, do something to make your mind strong, your body strong, and your spirit strong. If you are a healthy and balanced person, you can help to make the world a better place.

The story line for *Seven Wheels of Power* was inspired by several international traditions, particularly from Japan and India. The seven wheels on the Tree of Life are symbolic metaphors for the seven *chakras* on the body. According to some Hindu and yogic traditions, chakras are points along the body where energy connects and moves from the base of the spine to the top of the head. It is told that the seven chakras are disk shaped and, if seen, would each be a different color of the rainbow: red as the first chakra at the base of the spine, on up to violet as the seventh chakra at the crown of the head. It is also believed that if our chakras are out of balance, then we are not healthy. This is the source of the theme in the book that the Tree of Life will die if the wheels (chakras) are not in alignment.

Karate is a great way to get in better shape, to gain confidence, and to have fun! If you want to learn more about karate, check your local library, the Internet, or www.theblackbeltclub.com.

ABOUT THE AUTHOR

DAWN BARNES is a third-degree black belt and the founder of Dawn Barnes Karate Kids, the most successful all-children's karate school in the United States. She has taught martial arts to children for nearly twenty years, and she also writes columns for *Martial Arts Professional Magazine* and *Los Angeles Family Magazine*. As well, she is the Director of Children's Education for the National Association of Professional Martial Artists. Dawn lives in Los Angeles, California, with her family and two dogs. This is her first book.

ABOUT THE ILLUSTRATOR

BERNARD CHANG began his career in the comic book world, where his work on such popular characters including Doctor Mirage, Superman, and the X-Men earned him a coveted spot on the top ten artists in *Wizard: The Guide to Comics*. He is also a former Walt Disney Imagineer, designing concepts for theme parks, shows, and rides. He received his bachelor's degree in architecture from Pratt Institute in New York City, graduating with honors. Bernard lives in Los Angeles.

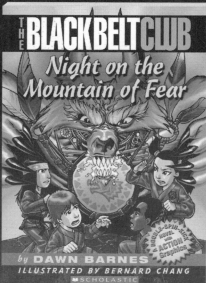